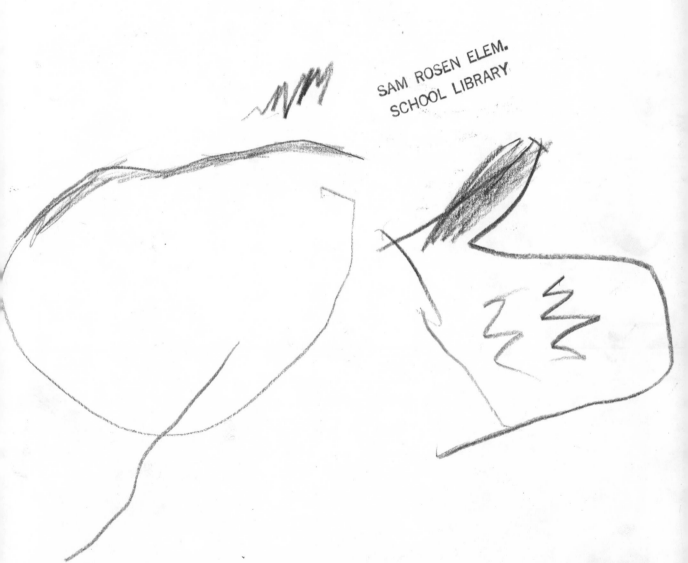

JULIE BRILLHART

Anna's Goodbye Apron

ALBERT WHITMAN & COMPANY, NILES, ILLINOIS

Library of Congress Cataloging-in-Publication Data
Brillhart, Julie.
Anna's goodbye apron /
story and pictures by Julie Brillhart.
p.   cm.
Summary: When a kindergarten class learns that
their teacher, Anna, is leaving, they decide
to make her an apron covered with drawings
to remember them by.
ISBN 0-8075-0375-4
[1. Teachers—Fiction. 2. Kindergarten—Fiction.
3. Schools—Fiction.] I. Title.
PZ7.B7666An   1990   89-49362
[E]—dc20   CIP
                                      AC

Text and illustrations © 1990 by Julie Brillhart.
Published in 1990 by Albert Whitman & Company,
5747 Howard Street, Niles, Illinois 60648.
Published simultaneously in Canada
by General Publishing, Limited, Toronto.
All rights reserved. Printed in the U.S.A.
10   9   8   7   6   5   4   3   2   1

Designer: Karen Johnson Campbell.
Illustrations are watercolor.
Type is set in Italia Book.

To Jeff, Jenny, Jake, and the Canterbury Children's Center.

Anna had been a teacher at the Canterbury Kindergarten for a long time. But now she had to move.

"I'm going to miss you all very much," she said to the children.

"I'm going to miss you, too," said Ethan.

"Me, too," said Laura. And they gave her a hug.

Anna had spent many happy days with the children
reading stories, painting pictures, and making letters and words.

She had taken them hiking through the woods and sledding down the hill.

They had visited a sheep farm and hugged the little lambs.

They had made animal puppets and put on a show
for the moms and dads.

And they had visited Anna's house! They had juice and crackers at her kitchen table and met Maggie, her dog.

"Boy, she's fat!" said Erica.

"You're right," said Anna. "She will be having her puppies soon."

What the children loved best was cooking. Anna had taught them to make all kinds of delicious treats—like dinosaur cookies, pretzels, and even real pizza!

One recipe they especially liked was "Anna's Popcorn Balls."
They loved to mix up the popcorn with syrup and pack it into balls.
It was fun—and tasted terrific!

Their favorite part came at the end
when they were cleaning up.

"Mmmm . . . this is yummy," said Amy.

"Next time, *I* get the bowl!" cried Sam.

Anna always laughed and said, "You are
the best bowl lickers I know!"

It was the week before Anna was supposed to leave.
On Anna's day off, her helper, Bill, suggested that the children
make a special goodbye present for Anna. It took them
a long time to decide what to make, but finally they all agreed.

They spent one whole morning working very hard
on the present. Finally, it was finished.

"Anna's going to love it!" said Bill.

All the children smiled.

Anna's last day had come, and it was time to give her the gift. Everyone gathered on the rug. The children were very excited.

Erica brought the present up to Anna. Anna very carefully
unwrapped the box and opened it up.

"WOW!" she cried. "This is wonderful!" She held up an apron that was decorated with bright, colorful pictures.

"We made it!" said Laura. "We drew the pictures!"

"All by ourselves!" added Amy.

"Try it on," said Ethan. Anna put the apron on. It fit just right and it looked good.

"YAY!" everyone cheered.

"Thank you very much," said Anna, smiling. "It's beautiful!"

Then Anna took the apron off and spread it on the rug.
The children crowded around her.

"This is the picture that *I* did," said Heidi. "That's you
and your dog, Maggie. Has she had her puppies?"

"Not yet," said Anna.

"This is mine," said Sam.
"I did a sun for you."

"I did this steam shovel,"
said William, "because
you know how much
I like digging machines
. . . and fire trucks!"

"Ethan and I did this one with all the flowers," said Amy. "They're lady slippers. Remember we saw some on our walk in the woods?"

"Yes," said Anna. "I remember. Oh—Matt. You must have done this one with the glasses. I'll never forget the first time you came to school wearing your new glasses. You were so nervous!"

"I know," said Matt. "Not anymore, though."

"Who did this brontosaurus standing on its head?" asked Anna.
"I did," said Brenda. "He's taking a nap!" Everyone laughed.

The rest of the children took turns showing Anna their pictures.

"This is the best present you could have given me," said Anna. "I'm going to miss you all very much. But every time I wear my apron, I will think of the fun we had together, and that will make me happy."

The children gave Anna a big, big hug.

Everyone felt very sad.

Now it was time for the children to go home.
Anna and Bill helped them get ready.
"I'm going to write you a letter," said Laura.

"Me, too," said Sam.

"That would be great!" said Anna. "I would like that."

The children waved goodbye to Anna. And Anna waved back.

A few weeks passed, and one morning a package
arrived at the kindergarten. It was from Anna!
Bill helped the children open it up.

Inside was a big, round tin full of cookies. On top of the tin was a letter. It said,

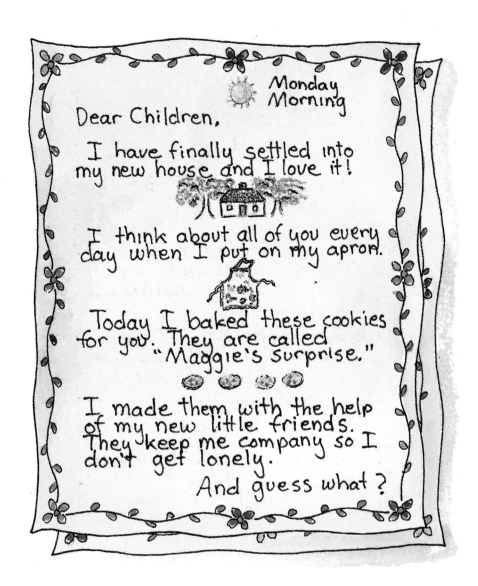

Monday Morning

Dear Children,

I have finally settled into my new house and I love it!

I think about all of you every day when I put on my apron.

Today I baked these cookies for you. They are called "Maggie's surprise."

I made them with the help of my new little friends. They keep me company so I don't get lonely.

And guess what?

They are great bowl
lickers, too!

Love, Anna